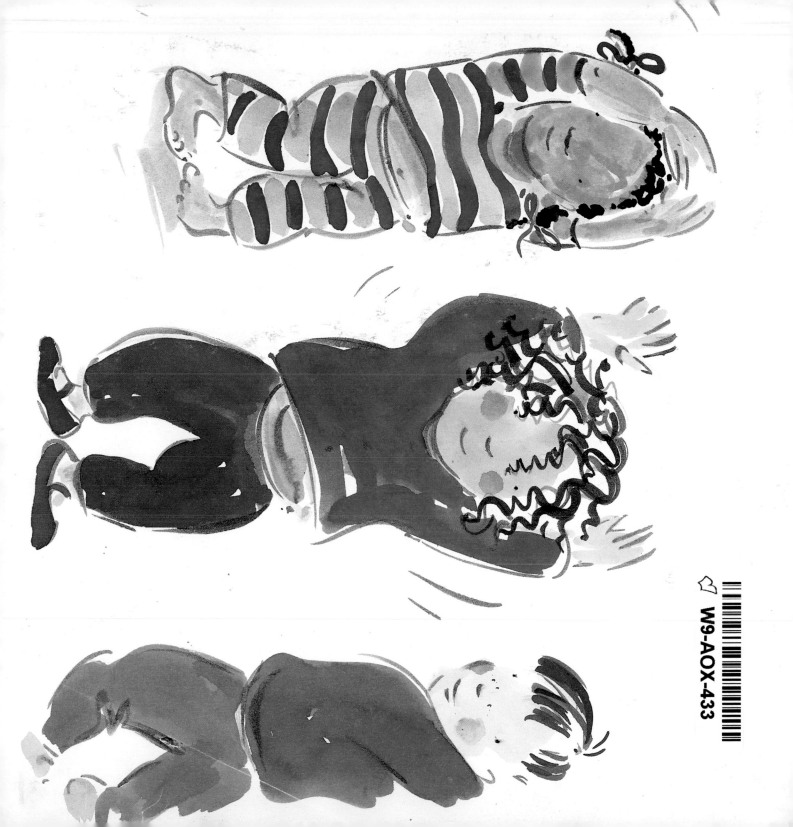

W9-AOX-433

To Loni and Josha

VIKING
Published by the Penguin Group
Viking Penguin, a division of Penguin Books USA Inc.,
375 Hudson Street, New York, New York 10014, U.S.A.
Penguin Books Australia Ltd, Ringwood, Victoria, Australia
Penguin Books Canada Ltd, 10 Alcorn Avenue, Toronto, Ontario, Canada M4V 3B2
Penguin Books (N.Z.) Ltd, 182–190 Wairau Road, Auckland 10, New Zealand

First published in Great Britain in 1992 by ABC, All Books for Children,
a division of The All Children's Company Ltd.

First American edition published in 1992

1 3 5 7 9 10 8 6 4 2
Copyright © Lucy Dickens, 1992
All rights reserved

Library of Congress Catalog Card Number: 91-50800
ISBN: 0-670-84484-5
Printed in Hong Kong

Without limiting the rights under copyright reserved above, no part of this
publication may be reproduced, stored in or introduced into a retrieval system,
or transmitted, in any form or by any means (electronic, mechanical, photocopying,
recording or otherwise), without the prior written permission of both
the copyright owner and the above publisher of this book.

2/18/13   CO23   14--

Dancing Class

LUCY DICKENS

Viking

"Oh, good, Laura, you're just in time. We're about to start class."

"All right, class, let's put our heels together. A little closer, Laura."

'Now we *march* two, three,
four, and *march*, two, oops!

Careful, Laura—don't step on Sam."

'Now we'll take turns tiptoeing like a fairy. Good, Daisy.'

"S-T-R-E-T-C-H, as tall as houses! Watch out, Mathew!"

"Can everyone touch their toes?
Careful, Mathew!"

'Heel and toe and heel and toe . . . .

. . . . and slide . . . .

. . . slide, slide, slide!"

"Let's see you fly just like a bird.
Open your eyes, Annie!"

"Now race like a train.
Hang on, caboose!"

"Ring–around–the–rosy . . ."

"Good work, class.
See you next week!"